MARVEL
CAPTAIN MARVEL
STARFORCE
MISSION LOG

fun
studio
INTERNATIONAL

My name is **Vers**, or so I've been told. That's what I go by anyway. I actually don't remember who I am. I don't remember where I was born, or how old I am. I don't remember who my parents are, or who my friends were. I don't remember anything before 6 years ago.

I lost my memory after the Kestelian attacks by the Skrulls, but I don't remember that either. That's why I began this mission log, to have a record of Vers, a journal written by my hand—just in case it happens again.

Since the time of my memory loss, I've begun my training to become a great Kree fighter. I joined an elite team called **Starforce** to help take down all galactic threats to the Kree empire.

Starforce is a special forces unit comprised of top-level Kree warriors—the best of the best! We're just a small group of six, but we each bring something special to the battlefield.

Bron-Char

is our team's muscle. He's HUGE and ridiculously strong. His biceps are probably as big as my thighs and he could probably squeeze open a can of food with his bare hands. I'm not kidding! He's also got a sharp mind and is easily the funniest member of the team—after me, of course!

Att-Lass

is our stealth infiltration specialist. His favorite weapons are his twin pistols. We've developed a strong bond and are almost like brother and sister, which is good because I've seen what he can do to people who make him mad.

ATT-LASS

KORATH

Korath is our team's second in command. His go-to weapons are his twin energy swords, which he carries on his back. He's an amazing fighter, he's just . . . too serious all of the time. I mean, I don't think this guy has ever smiled in his entire life, let alone laughed. That being said, I've decided to make it my personal mission to try and see if I can get him to crack.

Minn-Erva is our reliable

sniper, the only other woman on the team, and her marksmanship is incredible. She really doesn't like me though. Att-Lass told me that she used to be our leader's, Yon-Rogg's favorite, but now she believes I've replaced her as his personal number-one member of Starforce. I can't deny that Yon-Rogg and I have grown close, but she should learn to trust me. After all, we're on the same team!

MINN-ERVA

Yon-Rogg

is our fearless leader. As the head of team Starforce, what he says goes. It's his duty as first in command to not only brief us before our missions, but also to give orders on the battlefield. Being the highest-ranking officer in our unit is a huge responsibility, and Yon-Rogg is the **BEST KREE WARRIOR** for the job.

He has also become a great mentor, coach, and friend to me as I started my new life post-amnesia. Yon-Rogg was personally given the task to turn me into a first-class fighter. He's filled with a ton of **EXPERIENCE** and valuable **WISDOM**. I look to him for guidance, though I sometimes disagree with the knowledge that he tries to impart on me. I admit, I can be pretty stubborn on occasion. It's just that my gut instinct is always getting in the way, so I come off as defiant when I don't mean to. Maybe I can work on that so I can get along better with others on Starforce.

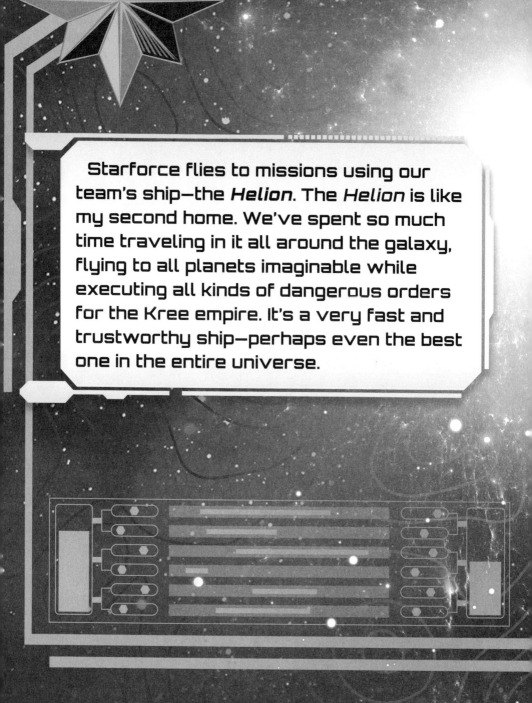

Starforce flies to missions using our team's ship—the *Helion*. The *Helion* is like my second home. We've spent so much time traveling in it all around the galaxy, flying to all planets imaginable while executing all kinds of dangerous orders for the Kree empire. It's a very fast and trustworthy ship—perhaps even the best one in the entire universe.

Helion

The Kree empire is vast. There are many planets that Starforce protects within the empire, but arguably the most important is the capital of the Kree dominion—Hala.

Hala is the main base of operations for Starforce and the entire team lives here. It's a wondrous place to live—a bustling mega-city with towering skyscrapers, speeding metro lines, and flying cars. I never get tired of admiring all its beauty!

Hala is home to millions of Kree—
a race of blue-, brown-, or beige-
skinned people. The people of
Hala display great deference to all
members of Starforce. As the Kree's
top military team, being charged with
defending its people is a tremendous
honor—one that the citizens of the
Kree Empire value, honor, and respect.

Starforce helps defend the Kree
from many galactic threats. Our
oldest battle is the Kree-Nova War.
It's a battle that has been going on for
centuries between the Kree Empire
and the Xandarians.

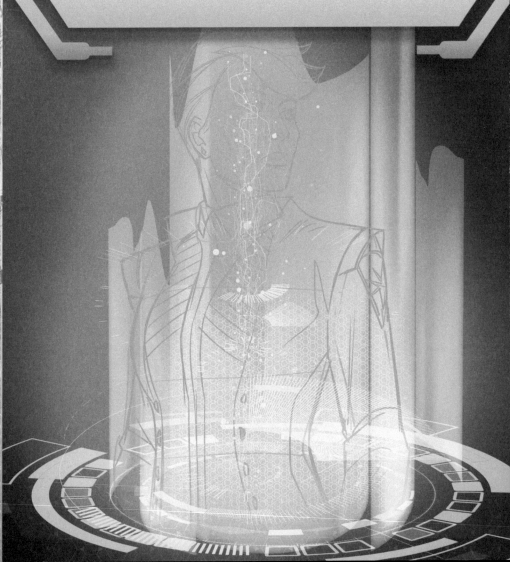

Xandar's military are called the Nova Corps—an intergalactic police force and space militia. Led by **Nova Prime**, the Nova Corps are a surprisingly honorable bunch of warriors. They generally use their words as a first line of defense before striking down their enemies.

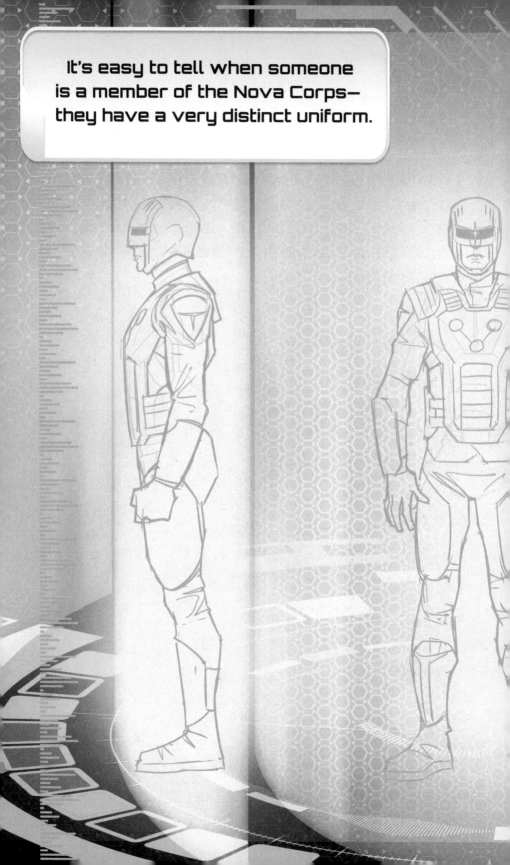

It's easy to tell when someone is a member of the Nova Corps—they have a very distinct uniform.

With pointed ears, a prominent jaw, and green skin, Skrulls are a scary-looking alien race, but even scarier than the way they look is their ability to shapeshift into anyone! They don't even need to touch their target to do it. They can morph into their chosen subject simply by looking at them!

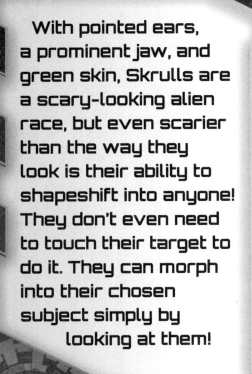

When a Skrull has shapeshifted—or simmed—into someone else, they are not only able to match DNA and other genetic markers, they are also able to recall the most recent memories of their target body. That makes it very difficult to tell if someone is really your friend, or a Skrull in disguise!

WAR

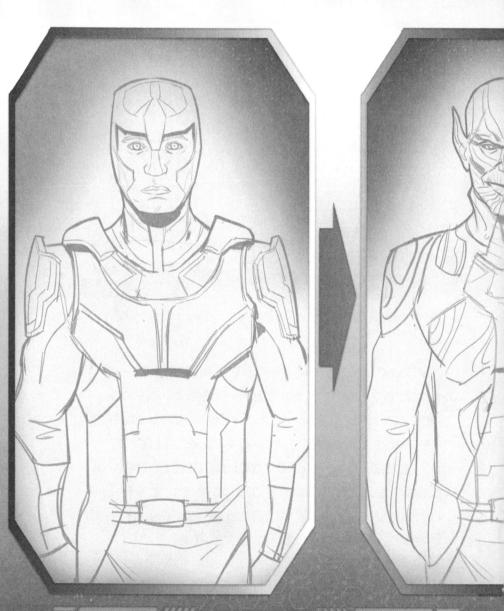

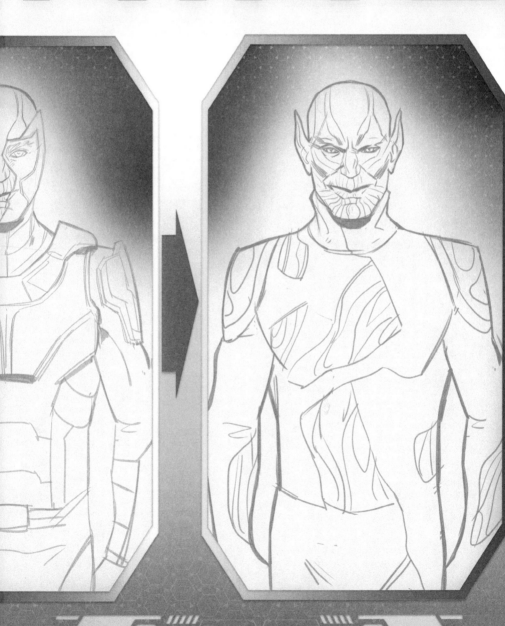

While the Xandarians are a formidable threat, and have been for centuries, our greatest enemy are the

Skrulls...

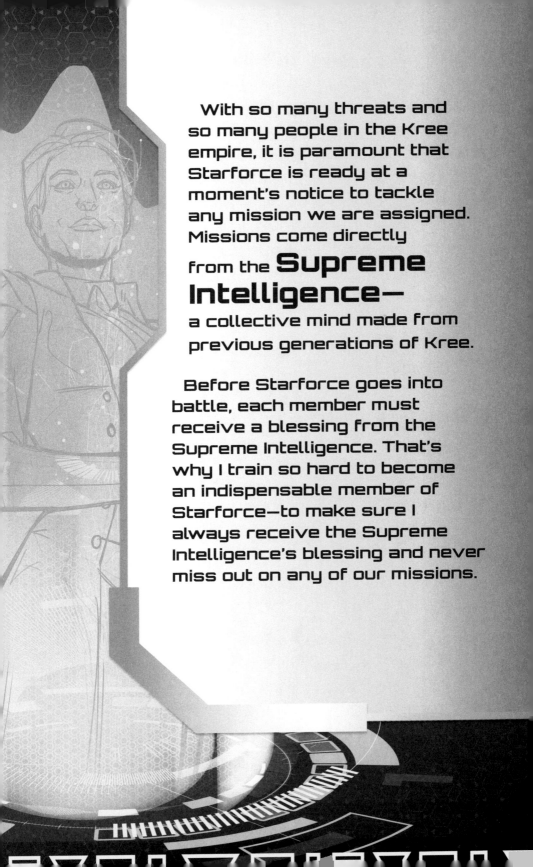

With so many threats and so many people in the Kree empire, it is paramount that Starforce is ready at a moment's notice to tackle any mission we are assigned. Missions come directly from the **Supreme Intelligence—** a collective mind made from previous generations of Kree.

Before Starforce goes into battle, each member must receive a blessing from the Supreme Intelligence. That's why I train so hard to become an indispensable member of Starforce—to make sure I always receive the Supreme Intelligence's blessing and never miss out on any of our missions.

I often work out with Yon-Rogg to make sure I am in top shape. I usually wake him up at his apartment, but today he was already waiting for me, anticipating my arrival. We quickly ran to our usual spot for our one-on-one training sessions—an old and simple-looking Kree gym. It doesn't have a lot of the amenities that some of the newer gyms have, but Yon-Rogg always says all we need are our minds and a mat, so when you look at it from his perspective, this gym is perfect.

Yon-Rogg primarily trains me to use my mental focus and hone my hand-to-hand combat skills. He wants to make sure I don't rely entirely on my superpowers.

Implanted under my left ear is a small metal disc. It's called a photon battery, and this disc is the source of my unique power. It was gifted to me by the Supreme Intelligence. It is the strength of the Supreme Intelligence that is transmitted into the battery. No other Kree warriors have been given one to channel their power except for me. I don't know why I was chosen, but I am honored nonetheless.

My abilities are like no other! I have superhuman strength, can make my fists glow, and can fire photon blasts—a type of supernatural light energy—from my fists, too! I wouldn't want to be on the receiving end of one of those, but I enjoy giving Yon-Rogg a taste of them when he pins me on the mat or ends up giving me a nosebleed during training. Photon energy is unbelievably powerful! While those are the only abilities I know how to use so far, I'm confident there are new powers just waiting for me to uncover.

After today's training session with Yon-Rogg, there was a Starforce team meeting where we were debriefed on our next mission. We learned that the Supreme Intelligence was working on a potential peace treaty to end the ongoing war with the Xandarians, which would allow us to conserve more resources and warriors for the ultimate battle against the Skrulls.

Although the peace treaty negotiations have been raised, the Kree military are not currently in a position of superiority—part of the reason the battle has remained ongoing—and part of the reason the Kree do not currently want to sign a treaty. To make sure the Kree are stronger before signing any treaty, it has been decided that Starforce will steal plans for a Xandarian weapon that would put the Kree in a more powerful position once the fighting has halted.

Our mission wasn't going to be easy. The plan was as follows:

>> Enter Xandarian occupied territory undetected by using one of their aircraft

>> Land on the Xandarian occupied planet, Sy'gyl

>> Make contact with a possible Xandarian defector

>> Find and obtain plans for a Xandarian weapon currently in development

>> Bring both the defector and the weapon plans back to Hala

We were told more details would be revealed once we were on Sy'gyl's surface.

Finally, Yon-Rogg let us know that we had all received the blessing of the Supreme Intelligence for this objective ahead of time, so we were all ready to go—and with that we were dismissed to prepare for the mission.

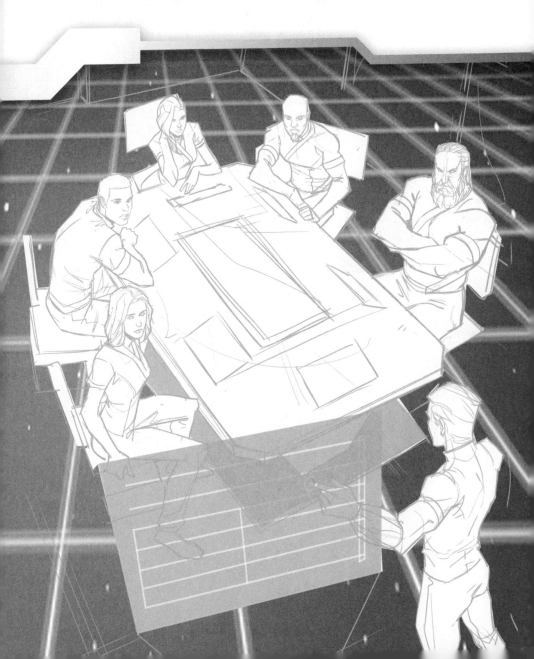

Once the gathering concluded, Minn-Erva asked what was bothering me—but the way she said it, I could tell she really didn't care, she was just doing it to rile me up. When I pressed her on the question, Minn-Erva said she was "just wondering when I was going to slip up."

I basically told her it was never going to happen. She has some nerve! Then she made some snarky remarks to the other guys on the team. After that, I REALLY wanted to show her what my photon blasts could do to her face, but I remembered what Yon-Rogg has been teaching me at our training sessions and I decided against it—lucky for her.

I don't think Minn-Erva will ever like me, but I'm past the point of caring.

Once I put on my combat uniform, I headed to the ship hangar where I was confronted with our ride to Sy'gyl—a battered and rickety old Xandarian freighter. It was clear the ship had some stories to tell. I understand the need for a ship to help us sneak into deep Xandarian territory, but was this really the best they could find? It looks like it would fall apart on takeoff.

Looking the ship over, it was then that I noticed someone I had never seen before—a Kree woman with short black, cropped hair. I learned from Korath that her name is Sun-Val and she would be our pilot for the mission. With a deep knowledge of Xandarian territory, she was to be treated as one of team Starforce.

Once we were finally ready to head to Sy'gyl, we chanted "for the good of the Kree" as is our tradition before departing Hala on all of our missions.

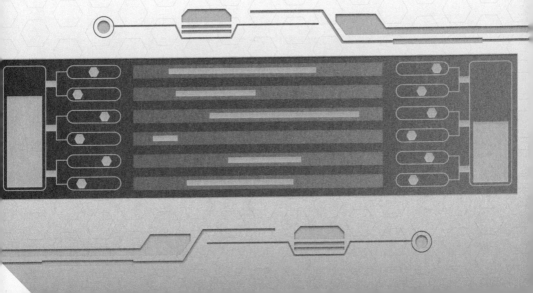

Leaving Hala's atmosphere on the Xandarian freighter was rough. The inside had been gutted to maximize the flight speed—anything that wasn't 100% necessary for the journey was ripped out. That included everything from padding and insulation, to seats. We had nowhere to sit on this beat-up thing! Instead, we were strapped to the inside panels of the craft. It was quite an uncomfortable experience, not to mention a noisy one with nothing to help absorb the vibrations.

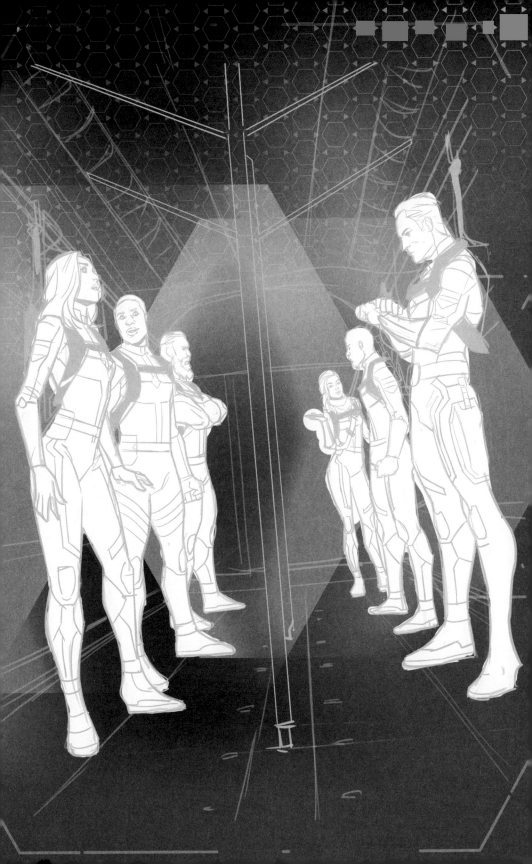

Once we were outside of Hala's atmosphere and Sun-Val was piloting the ship for Sy'gyl, we all unstrapped ourselves from the walls and received a more in-depth briefing from Yon-Rogg.

Korath and I were shown a holographic map of the compound that we needed to infiltrate—or rather that I needed to infiltrate. As soon as Yon-Rogg said it, I thought it was a mistake. Att-Lass was our infiltration specialist and the best at sneaking into structures undetected. Why was it supposed to be me this time?

When I asked Yon-Rogg why, he said that the order came from "the highest level." He didn't say it outright, but it could only mean one thing—the Supreme Intelligence.

Right before entering Xandarian-controlled space, our ship was attacked. So much for being incognito in our Xandarian ship. We had exchanged IDs and registration numbers with the Nova Corps, so there should be no reason they would fire at us unless they somehow knew we weren't who we said we were. Who else would be firing at us?

Quickly, we were told to strap ourselves against the panels of the ship. It was at this moment we all relied on the unknown Kree pilot, Sun-Val. We watched her attempt to outmaneuver the ships attacking her, but the freighter she was piloting wasn't designed for this kind of tactical evasion.

Flipping and diving, Sun-Val pulled on the controls furiously, trying to keep us out of harm's way.

With the ship finally in Xandarian galactic territory, Sun-Val easily piloted the battered ship toward Sy'gyl, landing the ship with ease.

Soon, we found ourselves on the boundary of an unpopulated region on Sy'gyl—a mountainous area with a fortress-like structure right in the middle of a crater. As soon as I saw the crater, I knew that was where we were headed.

With our bearings in place, it was time to obtain the plans for the Xandarian weapon, and it was up to Sun-Val to patch up the Xandarian freighter so we could all fly back home.

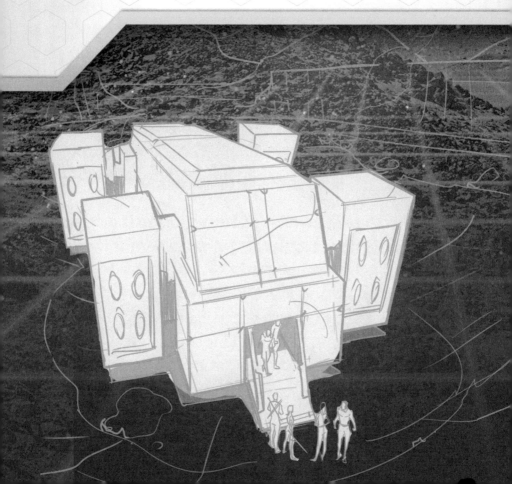

Sy'gyl is a dreadfully hot planet—temperatures ranging from ninety to one hundred twenty degrees Fahrenheit. With an unstable core at the planet's center, it was a literal hot-bed for earthquakes, volcanic eruptions, and geysers. Hot gas with a uniquely pungent odor seeped through small cracks in the ground, while small flames burst through the tiny fissures as well. We will need to be careful and avoid such hot spots.

While assessing the immediate perimeter, Att-Lass heard a sound and went off to investigate. He came back reporting that a Xandarian ship belonging to the Nova Corps was nearby. We were not alone.

Entering the bunker, I was shocked to discover it was mostly empty and filled with a smoky gas that made my eyes water. It was so thick I could barely see a few feet in front of me. I wouldn't let that stop me, though. I needed to make my way down to the third floor.

Creeping through the building, I kept wondering where all the Xandarians were. It was eerie. Nobody was there. Sometimes, it felt like someone was following me, but those feelings passed soon enough.

I reached a seemingly endless hallway with what seemed like hundreds of doors. I opened door after door, searching for Peer Kaal and the plans, but each turned up empty. Eventually, I stood before the last closed door. If Peer Kaal was not hiding behind it, I would fail my mission.

Throwing those thoughts aside as quickly as they came into my head, I closed my eyes in the hope that what I searched for was on the other side. Grabbing the knob, I gave it a turn, and pushed the final door open . . .

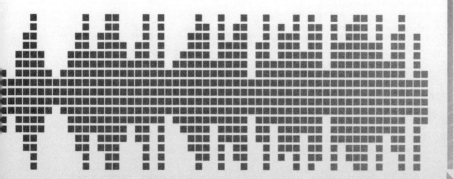

On the other side of the door, I spotted someone hiding in the shadows. Approaching the figure, I was able to make out the face of Peer Kaal—looking just like the photograph Yon-Rogg had given me. She stood there, and appeared to have been expecting me, which I found odd. I asked her for the plans, to which she answered, "I am the plans."

Not quite understanding what Peer Kaal was saying, I pressed her again. She told me that the plans for the Xandarian weapon, called an axiom cannon, were inside her head—or used to be anyway. She handed me a data capsule attached to a chain, which she said had a recording of her memories that included the plans for the axiom cannon. I quickly placed the data capsule around my neck and tucked it inside the top of my uniform.

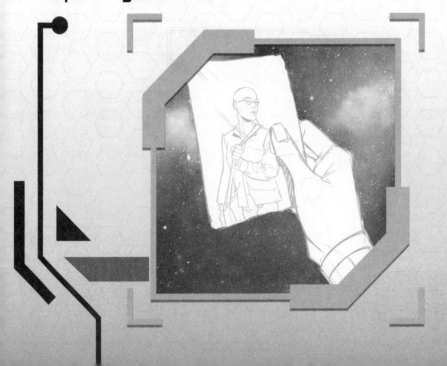

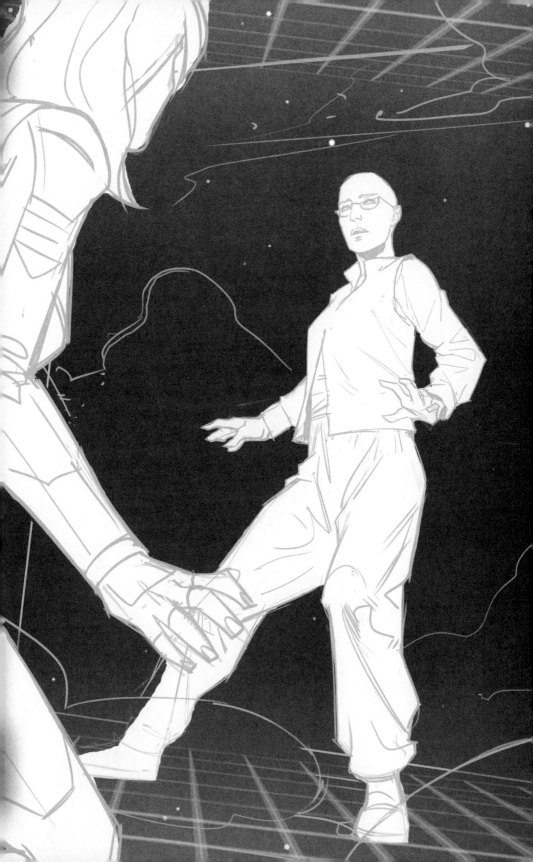

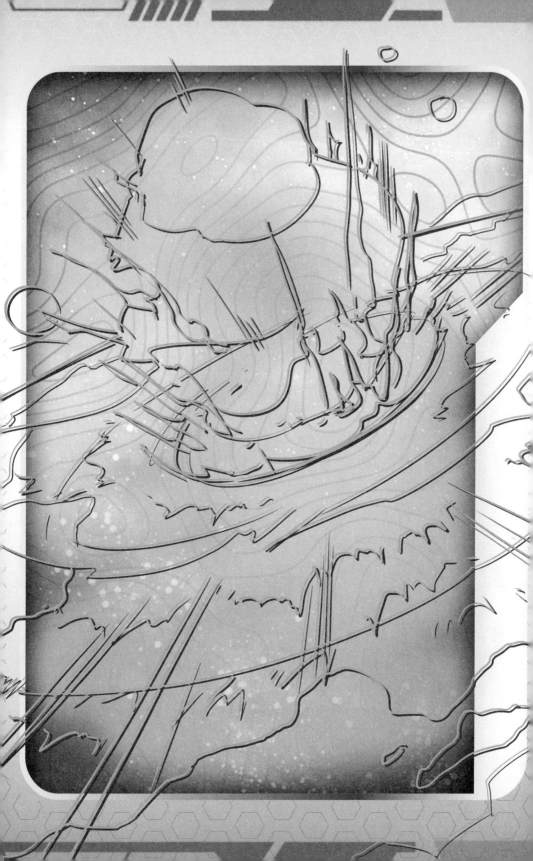

Peer Kaal then proceeded to tell me what the axiom cannon is capable of—destruction on a massive scale. She said that Sy'gyl used to be a planet covered with trees and flowers before the Xandarians tested out her weapon on the planet—changing it from a world of green to a world of fire. The earthquakes, volcanoes, and lava were a direct result of using the weapon.

With the plans obtained, I tried to convince her to come with me, as that was also one of Starforce's mission objectives—to bring the defector back to Hala—but she didn't want to come. With all the destruction she was responsible for on Sy'gyl after testing the axiom cannon, she didn't feel that she deserved a second chance—that she would never be able to atone for what she had not only created, but destroyed in the process.

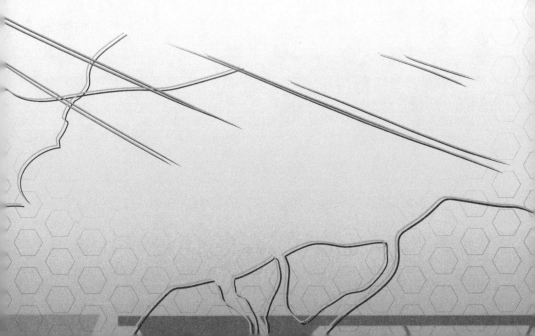

Peer Kaal refused to come back with me, but knowing that retrieving the plans for the axiom cannon was the primary objective, I had all I needed to make this mission a success. As I readied myself to return to the rest of Starforce, I heard someone behind me, there was no question this time.

Before I had a chance to turn and confront the individual, a hot metal object sliced deep into my right leg. Trying to comprehend what was going on, I turned just enough to see who stabbed me—a Xandarian woman dressed in Nova Corps gear, still holding the knife.

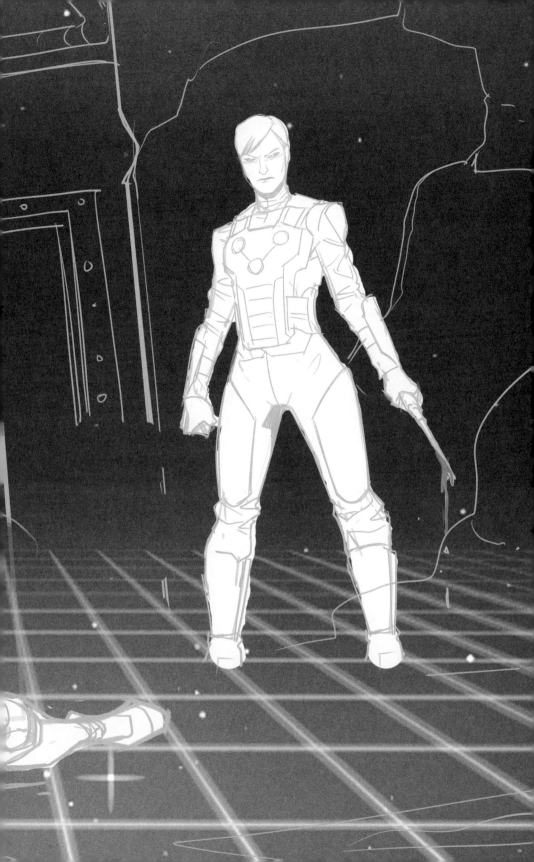

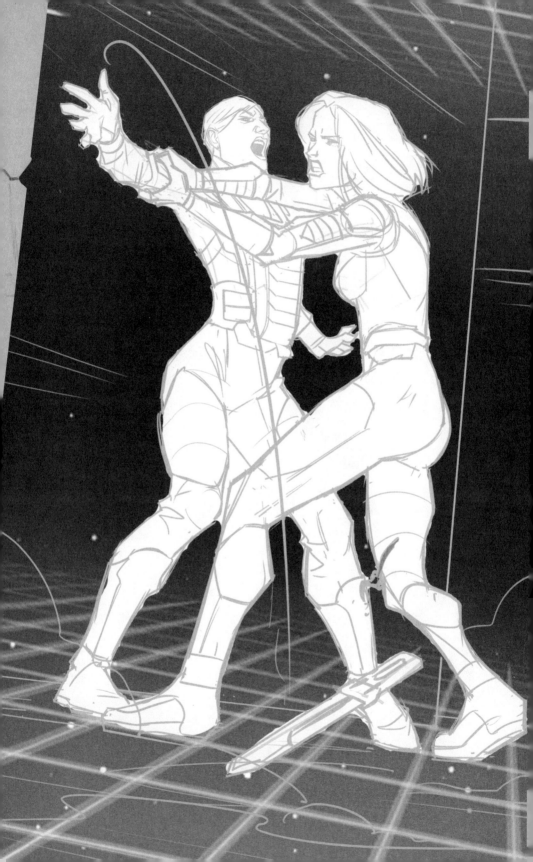

I quickly stood up, completely numb to the pain coming from the six-inch gash radiating from my leg. I lunged at my attacker and grabbed her fist that was holding the knife with both of my hands. Using my brute strength, I slammed her hand over and over again into a nearby wall to try and get her to release her hold. Finally, she let go of the knife, dropping it to the ground.

After the threat of the knife was removed, I struggled with my assailant, trying to quickly gain the upper hand. Using a move that Yon-Rogg taught me the last time we went to the gym, I flipped the Xandarian woman over my shoulder and placed her in a choke hold. I was mere moments away from knocking her unconscious, when out of nowhere, a faint whistling sound could be heard steadily getting louder. I recognized that sound. Something was incoming, and there was no time to run. Suddenly, the building exploded.

Miraculously pulling myself from the rubble, Peer Kaal and the Xandarian warrior were nowhere to be found. I could only presume the worst. I kept thinking about the Xandarian woman in the Nova Corps gear. Her actions didn't scream "Nova." They tended to operate under a code of conduct. The fact that she snuck up behind me and used a knife was not typical.

While trying to make sense of my assailant, a shooting pain rang out from my leg. I looked down to my right side to see a stream of blue flowing freely from the gash. I knew I needed to stop the bleeding— and FAST! Tearing a piece of fabric from my uniform, I tied it around my leg above the open wound and pulled it tight to stop the bleeding—creating a makeshift tourniquet. It didn't stop all of the bleeding, but helped stop the flow enough. It would buy me more time to get back to the extraction point.

With my leg taken care of—at least to the best of my abilities—I tried standing on it, but each time I put pressure on it, I couldn't help but cry out in pain. Knowing that standing on both legs was not an option, I began to drag my injured one behind me. I had to try and find a way to escape the rubble.

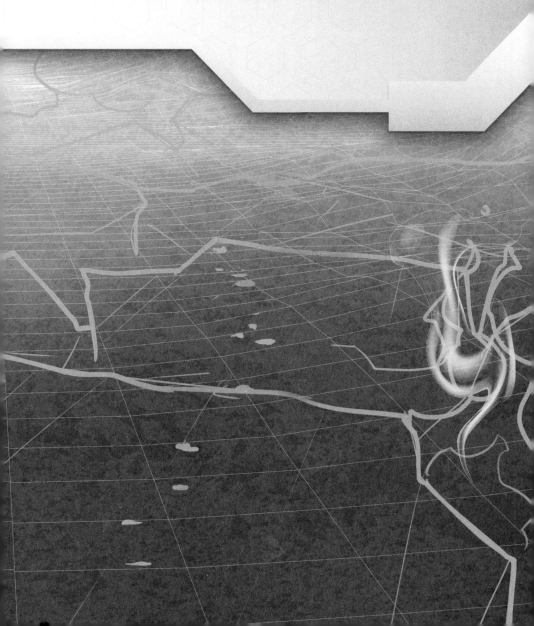

Hobbling through the ruins, I noticed a trail of blue blood behind me. My wound was giving away my escape path. Knowing that the "Nova" woman, or other potential enemies, could discover the blood trail gave me pause. I hoped no one would find the clue and trace that I was here. With my leg in its current state, outrunning any threat I might encounter was not an option.

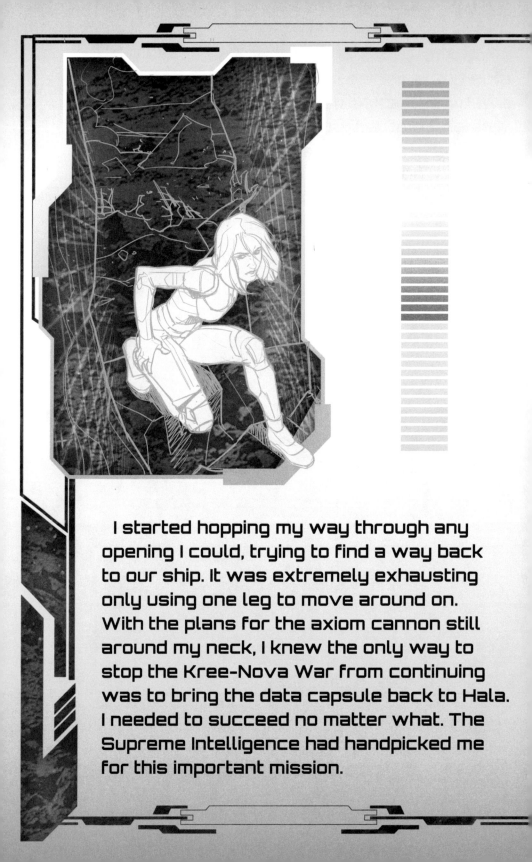

I started hopping my way through any opening I could, trying to find a way back to our ship. It was extremely exhausting only using one leg to move around on. With the plans for the axiom cannon still around my neck, I knew the only way to stop the Kree-Nova War from continuing was to bring the data capsule back to Hala. I needed to succeed no matter what. The Supreme Intelligence had handpicked me for this important mission.

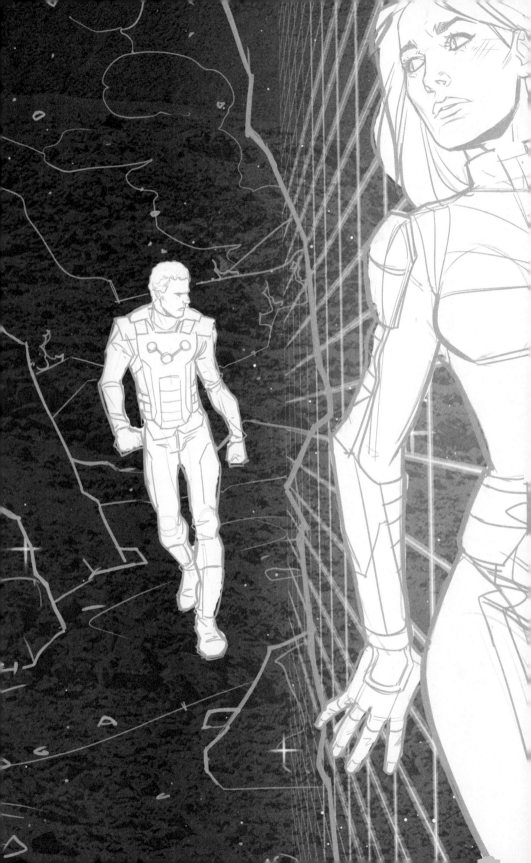

After hobbling some distance, I heard a sound coming from around the corner. Someone was near. Was it the attacker from the bunker who stabbed me in my leg? Had she survived the blast?

I moved closer to the corner and peered around the edge. I spied the source of the sound—a man in a Nova Corps uniform with curly brown hair. He was quite tall, about six feet high, and had a stocky build. Unable to move quickly to avoid a confrontation, I prepared for one head-on. I held my breath as I waited for the approaching footsteps to move closer . . . closer . . . closer . . .

As soon as he appeared, I grabbed him in a choke hold. I started squeezing as hard as I could to make him pass out, but he was tougher than he looked. With my arm still wrapped around his neck, he struggled to speak with me. "I'm not here to hurt you," he sputtered, "I can get you out of here alive."

I told him how I was attacked by someone wearing a Nova uniform, and pressed him for details. He didn't know who had attacked me, but he said it wasn't him—he came alone. I wasn't sure why, probably my instinct stepping in, but I believed him, so I let go of my grip.

After catching his breath, the man told me his name was Rhomann Dey and that he was a corpsman in the Nova Corps. He said he was sent to help me, which greatly confused me as our provinces are at war with each other. I asked him what he knew about the earlier explosion. He stated that he didn't know who did it, but that the Nova Corps wasn't involved.

Dey then said that he knew I was there to steal the plans for the axiom cannon, and that he was there to make sure I succeeded. He had direct orders from Nova Prime herself, believing that if both sides have the same technology, there will be balance for peace to exist between us. With opposition among some Xandarians, she couldn't give the plans to the Kree outright, so this was the next best thing.

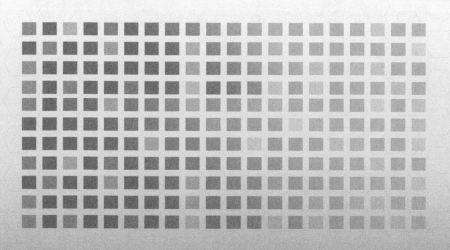

Dey said we had to move, so I began hobbling again, trying to keep up. He offered to help me, but I'm too proud and stubborn to accept. I always feel like I need to do things on my own. My leg kept feeling worse, and I was still losing some blood.

We finally made our way out from the rubble to a nearby forest. From that point, I knew we were only three clicks away from reaching the extraction zone.

Seeing the damage to my limb, Corpsman Dey said we needed to take care of my leg, otherwise I wasn't going to make it. He stated he was trained in combat medicine and could help. I didn't really want him touching my leg because I didn't fully trust him, but I figured he could have killed me multiple times by now, so I at least felt he wasn't going to end my life then and there. I had that much confidence in him at that point.

I sat down on the ground so he could better assess my leg. As soon as he started working on it, I grew faint and suddenly passed out.

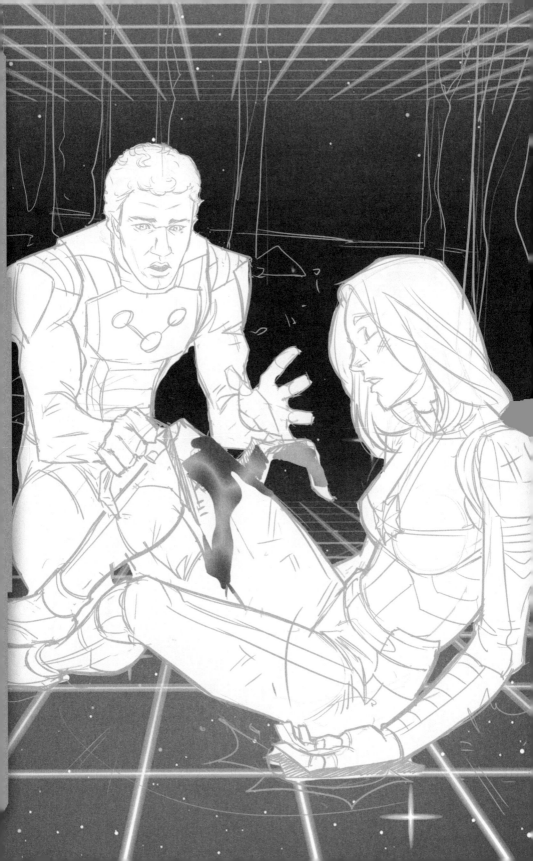

I woke up to Rhomann Dey staring at me. I instinctively reached toward my neck, searching for the chain holding the data capsule. It was still safely there.

Breathing a sigh of relief, I asked Dey how long I had been out. He said I had been unconscious for 15 minutes. During that time, he had replaced my tourniquet with a much better bandage, and gave me something for the pain.

I didn't have too much time to admire his work as we started to smell smoke. Fire had caught on some of the nearby trees. With the wind blowing in our direction, it wouldn't take long for the flames to reach us. We needed to get out of harm's way as quickly as possible.

Dey had a map of the area on his wrist communicator. He said if we made it to the edge of the forest we were currently in, we would find a rocky clearing where the fire couldn't get us. We decided to go there and then try and figure out the best way to get to my ship in order to reunite with my team.

Soon the woods were ablaze. Lava proceeded to burst out of the cracks in the ground like flaming geysers. We needed to watch our step. The axiom cannon had made Sy'gyl unstable, but the planet seemed particularly volatile at the moment.

Fire danced from treetop to treetop, slowly gaining upon on us. I hobbled along as Dey urged me on, knowing that the rocky clearing was just beyond the last group of trees, mere meters in front of us.

Barely keeping ahead of the flames, we emerged from the woods just as the last trees behind us were slowly engulfed. We had arrived in the rocky clearing. Completely exhausted and ready to take a break, I didn't see the imminent danger.

Before I knew what was going on, Dey pushed me to the ground with the entire force of his body. An energy blast hit the ground right next to us. Someone was firing directly at us. He told me to keep down and that we needed to seek cover.

We crawled over to a giant rock to protect us from the assailant's blasts. Once there, I looked up to the top of the ridge and saw a Xandarian soldier shooting at us. Dey was quick to say the man wasn't Nova, though I didn't quite understand how he knew. The soldier certainly looked like Nova, although his continuous firing made it hard to see him very well.

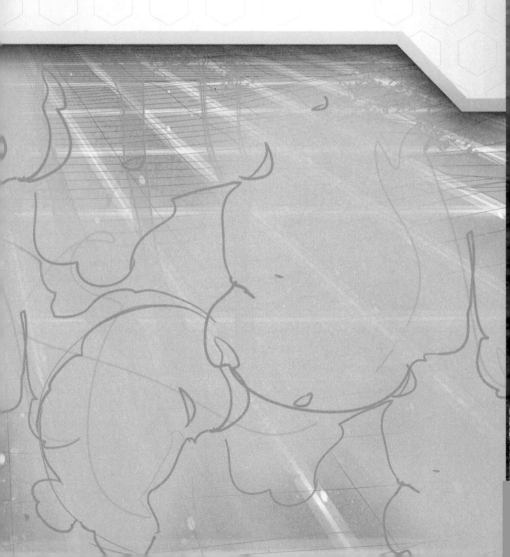

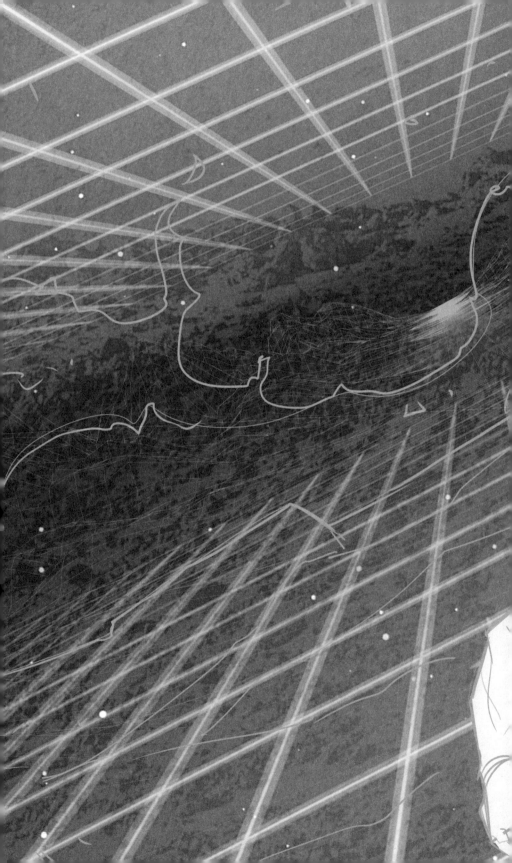

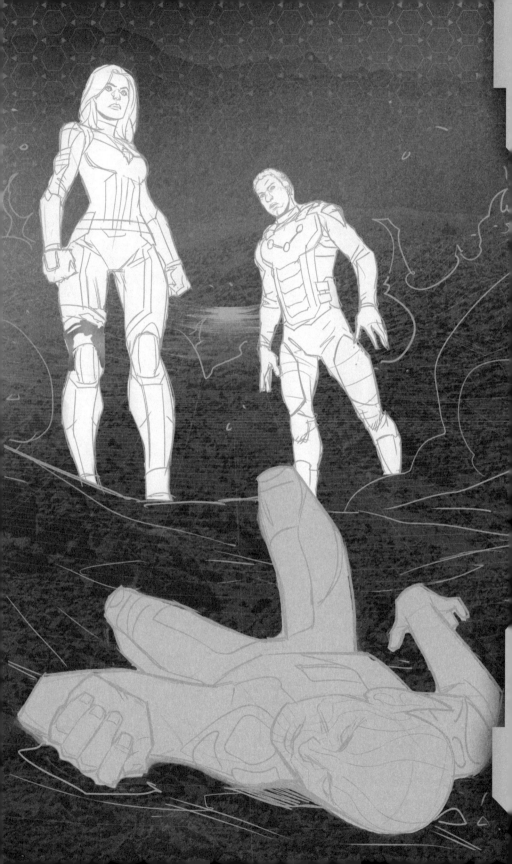

The energy blasts were endless. Since Dey and I didn't have any weapons on us, I knew there was only one thing to do. I started to gather energy in my fists and proton-blasted the shooter. The Xandarian warrior tumbled down the ridge and landed near us—weak, but alive.

Amazed by my power, Dey stood shocked.

I mused that if anyone was with this fighter, my display would have alerted them to our presence. Dey quipped back that they already knew. I pressed him for answers and he motioned toward the man that I recently grounded. We watched together as the man slowly started to change shape . . . into a green alien. The Xandarian warrior was actually a Skrull! His injuries from my photon blast made it tough for him to hold his simmed form. Now out cold, he wasn't going to hurt anyone for quite some time.

Dey wasn't shocked by this transformation at all. He said a few Skrulls arrived on Sy'gyl shortly before Starforce did. He was tracking them and knew there were two of them that had landed on the planet. If this was one of them, that meant there was one more hiding somewhere.

With the threat of Skrulls also on the planet, I knew I needed to get back to the extraction point stat. Dey and I quickly made our way across the rocky terrain. The trek was thankfully uneventful. Eventually, we reached a hill. I knew my ship and team were on the other side. As he couldn't come with me—since he was technically still my enemy— we began to exchange parting words.

While saying goodbye, Yon-Rogg, Korath, Bron-Char, and Sun-Val all emerged from some nearby trees. Apparently, we were talking a bit too loudly and they had heard us. They were thankful to know that I was still alive, and I was grateful that they hadn't assumed I died in the bunker explosion and left me for dead.

Now that I was reunited with my team, Yon-Rogg smiled at Rhomann Dey and let him know his mission was complete. Apparently, Yon-Rogg knew a bit more about this mission than he had let on in the beginning.

Objective now complete, Dey smiled back and walked straight back into the woods, disappearing from view.

With Dey gone, someone was quite eager to return to the freighter—Sun-Val. She kept trying to urge us back. I asked what she was doing out here, since I found it odd she wasn't with the Xandarian freighter she was tasked to repair.

Bron-Char explained that when we were all on our mission and Sun-Val was fixing the ship, she heard a nearby sound in the trees and went to investigate. They ran into her in the woods. Att-Lass and Minn-Erva should be back at the ship by now, so there was no need to worry about the ship being left unattended.

Yon-Rogg, Korath, Bron-Char, Sun-Val, and I climbed over the hill and emerged through the trees . . . right at the base of our craft. Almost as soon as we got there, Minn-Erva was there pointing her rifle directly at me. I knew she hated me, but this behavior seemed extreme.

Suddenly, she yelled my way,

"Get down!"

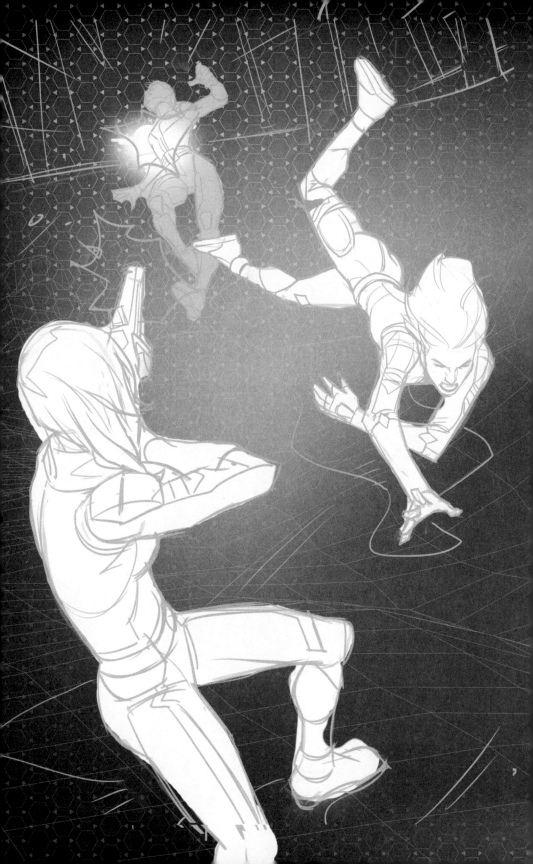

Without thinking, I dropped my body, hitting the ground so quickly that I was unable to catch myself—unintentionally twisting my right leg and injuring it even further on my way down. At that moment, Minn-Erva fired two shots from her rifle straight into the person who was behind me.

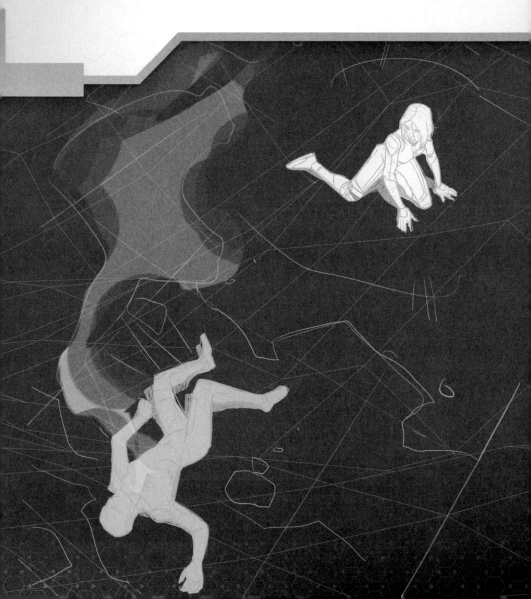

Sun-Val slumped down from the shots fired into her body. Suddenly, her face gradually changed, shifting into a Skrull. Sun-Val was a Skrull—the second one that Dey had mentioned earlier.

Minn-Erva and Att-Lass told us they had found the real Sun-Val's body when they were on their way back to our rendezvous point. When they saw the second Sun-Val emerging from the trees, they knew it was an imposter.

Pulling the data capsule's chain over my head, I handed it over to Yon-Rogg for safekeeping. These Skrulls—obviously here for the axiom cannon, too—would not be victorious in their goal. We had won. Our mission was **COMPLETE**. With these plans in the hands of the Kree, peace between our people and the Xandarians was now a real possibility.

Climbing back inside the Xandarian freighter, we started to head back home to Hala. I knew my leg would need some major work to get it back to how it used to be. Yon-Rogg told me to get some rest and that I was to go straight to the med-bay upon our return. That was an order.

Back on Hala, I went to the med-bay where my leg was attended to by the best Kree doctors. I was told it would be weeks before I could put any pressure on it, and that it would take even more time to regain the strength I had before I was stabbed.

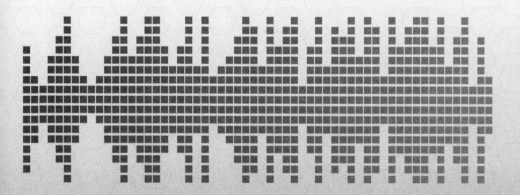

It's been quite some time since the mission to retrieve the plans for the axiom cannon. Since then, **peace has been reached between the Kree and the Xandarians, but the war between us and the Skrulls has only intensified.** Streets are littered with warnings about the Skrull's simming capabilities, and the Kree have every reason to fear what they can do.

Having experienced their abilities first-hand on Sy'gyl, I've intensified my training since then to make sure I'm ready for the next time I confront one.

I've been so focused on recuperating my right leg and pouring all my energy into strength training that I've been too exhausted at the end of the day to write much recently. This mission log is going to be different though, it's beyond any dangerous task or alien encounter I've ever experienced, up until now . . .

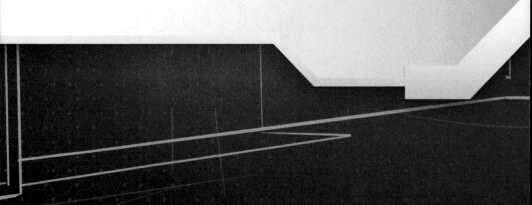

It happened again—the nightmare that occurs almost every night. It's always the same. Nothing new. I've had it so many times in the past six years that I can practically relive it simply by closing my eyes.

I'm piloting some type of jet in outer space above a beautiful blue planet. A copilot is sitting in the seat behind me, but I can never quite make out their face. Suddenly, alien blasts start streaming past my windshield. We're under attack! I start dodging the blasts, guiding the ship through an intricate series of spins and rolls. Eventually, one of the blasts hits our craft and we start spiraling out of control to the surface of some planet.

Once on the surface, I emerge from the ship, completely surrounded by fire. I try to rouse my copilot, but realize they didn't make it. As soon as I lift my head up, I see a shadowy green figure in the distance raising their blaster toward me and . . .

That's it, I always wake before a shot is fired. I can't seem to force myself to stay in the dream beyond this moment.

Is this a fragment from my past, or is it simply a creation sprung from the deepest corners of my mind? Some say dreams have meanings, but if so, I don't know what this one is trying to tell me.

Waking from my nightmares, I find relief in looking out the window of my apartment and realizing that I am safe at home on planet Hala. On these nights, it's hard for me to go back to sleep. I've taken to waking Yon-Rogg to train. I claim it's due to the injury I suffered on Sy'gyl, even though Yon-Rogg says I've fully recovered from it.

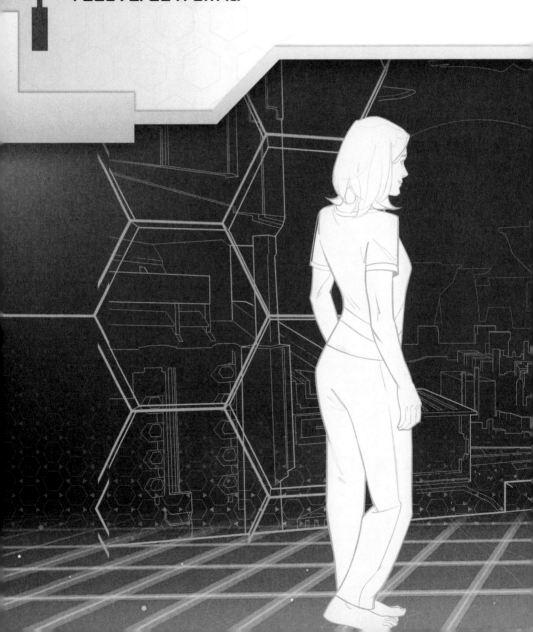

I knocked on his door and woke him up to go to the gym. I have to hand it to Yon-Rogg—even though he would rather sleep when I wake him, he always makes time for us to train. Sometimes I feel he is more dedicated to my training than I am.

After Yon-Rogg and I finished our training session today, we headed toward the Hala city metro to go back home. All around the station and inside the transit carriages are constant reminders that we are at war with the Skrulls. Animated posters alert the public to the dangers our enemy pose to our way of life.

It's part of the reason why Yon-Rogg is so revered by the citizens of Hala. He is a famous warrior in the fight against the Skrulls. Whenever Kree approach him or salute him to show their gratitude, he's always very gracious. I can only hope to be as admired as he is one day—not that I would ever admit that to him.

During the ride home, an alarm went off across the city, signaling our need to prepare for battle. I had initially hoped it was a drill, but we weren't that lucky. We quickly headed toward Upper Hala and into the Kree military tower to await the rest of the team.

Not much different from our last task but definitely riskier. Hopefully I avoid injury this time, too, but will I also be able to avoid another wisecrack from Minn-Erva?

We've been informed that Soh-Larr's cover was blown when he sent a warning signal back to Hala and that it was intercepted by the Skrulls. The enemy is now aware of Soh-Larr's presence on Torfa, so we need to find him before they do. Always easier said than done!

After our mission briefing, we headed toward the *Helion* to begin the journey: destination Torfa. Ever since our stealth mission to Sy'gyl when we had to fly aboard that decrepit Xandarian aircraft, I feel immense gratitude for the beauty and solid craftsmanship of our *Helion*. That previous hunk of junk was the WORST.

Waiting by our trusty craft was the high-ranking Kree commander **Ronan the Accuser**. Ready for our endeavor, we all chanted with him in unison, "for the good of the Kree." He decided to come out and wish all of us a safe mission. He's a pretty fierce and menacing figure to reckon with, so I'm glad he's on our side.

I've missed this ship so much. Thankfully the *Helion's* interior is in tip-top shape—navigation controls toward the front, where we pilot the ship, and our team's main central zone, where we spend the majority of our time in-flight. In that zone, we have some pod tables around the perimeter of the room, one for each team member, as well as hexagonal patterns on the floor that form a circle. When you stand on a hexagon, you are able to enter a virtual chamber where you can converse with the Supreme Intelligence—that same collective mind that gave me my unique photon battery.

Again—no warrior is allowed to enter battle without the blessing of the Supreme Intelligence. Sometimes Yon-Rogg receives the consent for us ahead of our missions, like on our latest Xandarian mission, but other times like this, we enter the virtual chamber to receive its consent ourselves. I'm always so nervous before entering the virtual chamber by myself. I really hope I get to go on this mission.

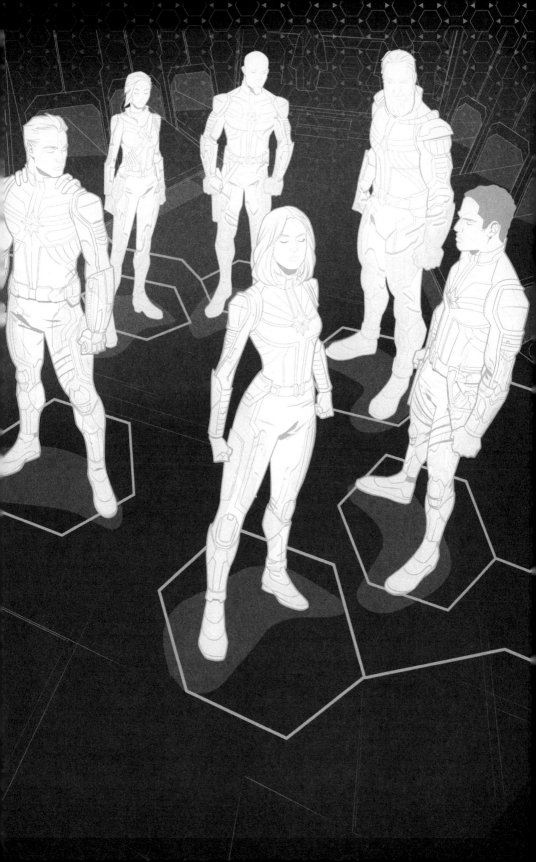

Meeting with the Supreme Intelligence is always a strange experience, and this time was no exception. No Kree knows the Supreme Intelligence's true form. Instead, our own subconscious chooses how they appear to each individual. That means the older woman I see when I enter the virtual chamber is someone that I've probably met in my real life—I just don't remember how, where, or when I've met the person they have modeled themselves after due to my memory loss.

I wish I could talk about this with someone and tell them who I see—maybe that would trigger some of my memories so I can remember my past—but what one sees in the virtual chamber is sacred, and personal, no Kree ever reveals what form they see.

This time, I tried asking the Supreme Intelligence who from my subconscious they were mimicking, but of course they wouldn't tell me. I wondered if the woman who appeared before me could be my mother. As usual, they gave me the blessing for the imminent mission and wished me good luck.

With all of Starforce having received a blessing from the Supreme Intelligence, we prepared for our arrival on Torfa. It wasn't long before we reached the planet's surface—a rocky terrain covered in a thick blanket of fog that appeared menacing as it masked the ancient Torfan ruins rising in the horizon. Soh-Larr's beacon signal was coming from one of those temples, so he was very close!

Touching our forearm consoles, we all changed from our traditional uniform colors to a camouflage pattern that blended perfectly with the current surroundings. It's so much easier to sneak around this way when you've come uninvited!

As we made our way toward the temple, Korath's sensor started to detect multiple lifeforms, but he couldn't discern what kind of lifeforms they were—Torfan or Skrull. Yon-Rogg told us to assume all life is a Skrull unless proven otherwise. We were to remain on high alert.

Knowing there were other lifeforms nearby, Yon-Rogg ordered us to spread out and get into position. Minn-Erva and Att-Lass were told to provide cover and hold their post on a nearby ridge, while the rest of us headed closer to the temple where Soh-Larr's signal was coming from.

Once we crossed over the ancient bridge leading us to the temple, we knew we would be encountering the lifeforms Korath's sensor had detected earlier. Suddenly, from the corner of my eye, I saw something move. I whisked around quickly and saw . . .

Torfans! A group of them huddled together and very afraid. They're such a gentle race of creatures. I'm sure my glowing fists frightened them greatly. After calming them down and signaling for them all to be quiet, we continued with our mission to rescue Soh-Larr.

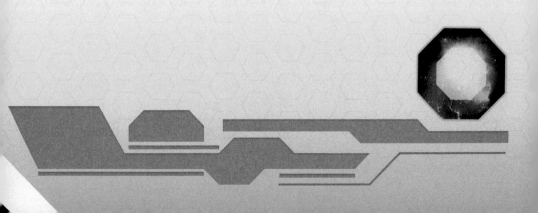

After crossing the bridge, we made it to the entrance of the temple. Bron-Char and Korath were told to keep watch outside while Yon-Rogg and I went inside to locate our target.

The temple's main chamber was dark, although it was somewhat easier to see in this room than through the dense fog outside. I called out to Soh-Larr to let him know it was safe to come out of the shadows, and he quickly appeared—a blue-skinned Kree covered in fresh scars that were evidence of recent torture.

I immediately asked Soh-Larr to recite a code that only he would know—one buried deep within his subconscious—to verify his identity and make sure he wasn't a Skrull in disguise. Without pause, Soh-Larr responded with the correct code, confirming he was our spy. Somehow, his delivery felt off, though I couldn't quite pinpoint why.

With the target acquired, we were ready to head back to Hala. As I tended to the injured Soh-Larr, a large bellowing sound could be heard from just beyond the temple's entrance—we recognized it to be the unnerving signal of a Skrull battle cry.

I quickly enabled the Starforce combat colors, grabbed Soh-Larr, and ran with him outside of the temple just in time to see thousands of "Torfans" turning into Skrulls. We were completely surrounded by our enemy. It was a trap!

We needed to get Soh-Larr back to the *Helion* and fast. Using my photon blasts, I attacked the Skrulls, trying to push a path back over the bridge. The other members of Starforce acted as our cover—Bron-Char, Korath, and Yon-Rogg had just finished battling their way through the ambush, helping to clear a path for us to follow.

Then, out of nowhere—BOOM!—an explosion went off, collapsing the end of the bridge and taking Soh-Larr and I down with it. Miraculously, we managed to grab onto a lower ledge, but there was no easy way out of this situation! The blast greatly injured Soh-Larr, and destroyed our most direct route back to the ship. I needed to hide him until we could find a different way out.

Soh-Larr was too weak, so I had to carry him into some cave-like tunnels tucked beneath the planet's surface. It was an ideal hiding spot and everything seemed to be okay. But Soh-Larr started asking me some strange questions and then . . . I felt a painful jolt run throughout my body. I was unable to move and completely paralyzed. Soh-Larr's injuries started to heal right before my eyes as he transformed into a green-skinned Skrull!

NOT AGAIN!

Laying there in that moment, I was angry with myself and wondered how I missed the signs that the "Soh-Larr" I was protecting was actually a Skrull. I blindly accepted it as fact when he recited the real Soh-Larr's verification code. I didn't listen to my instinct that something in that moment felt off.

Then the Skrull hit me with a stun device and everything went black. In that pitch-black, darkness I found myself thinking . . . contemplating . . . how I was going to get myself out of this one? Oddly enough, I wasn't too worried. I always find a way.